First published in North America
in 2019 by Boxer Books Limited.
www.boxerbooks.com
Boxer® is a registered trademark
of Boxer Books Limited.

Text copyright © 2019 Sam Williams
Illustrations copyright © 2019 Matt Hunt
The right of Sam Williams to be identified as the
author and Matt Hunt to be identified as the
illustrator of this work has been asserted by them
in accordance with the Copyright, Designs
and Patents Act, 1988.

The text is set in Verveine.
ISBN 978-1-912757-14-5

1 3 5 7 9 10 8 6 4 2

Printed in China
All of our papers are sourced from managed forests
and renewable resources.

For Orian
love from
Sam Williams x

For my family
Matt Hunt

# HOW ABOUT A NIGHT OUT?

by
Sam
Williams

Illustrated
by
Matt Hunt

Boxer
Books

Lap cats are lazy cats

Who only sleep on hallway mats.

Come out to play
on city nights.

Perhaps there'll
be an owl about?
Hooting about . . .

whoooo
knows
what!

We'll take turns
on the roundabout.

We'll
**SWOON**
to the moon
if the moon
is out.

We'll catercall upon the wall

And never worry if we fall.

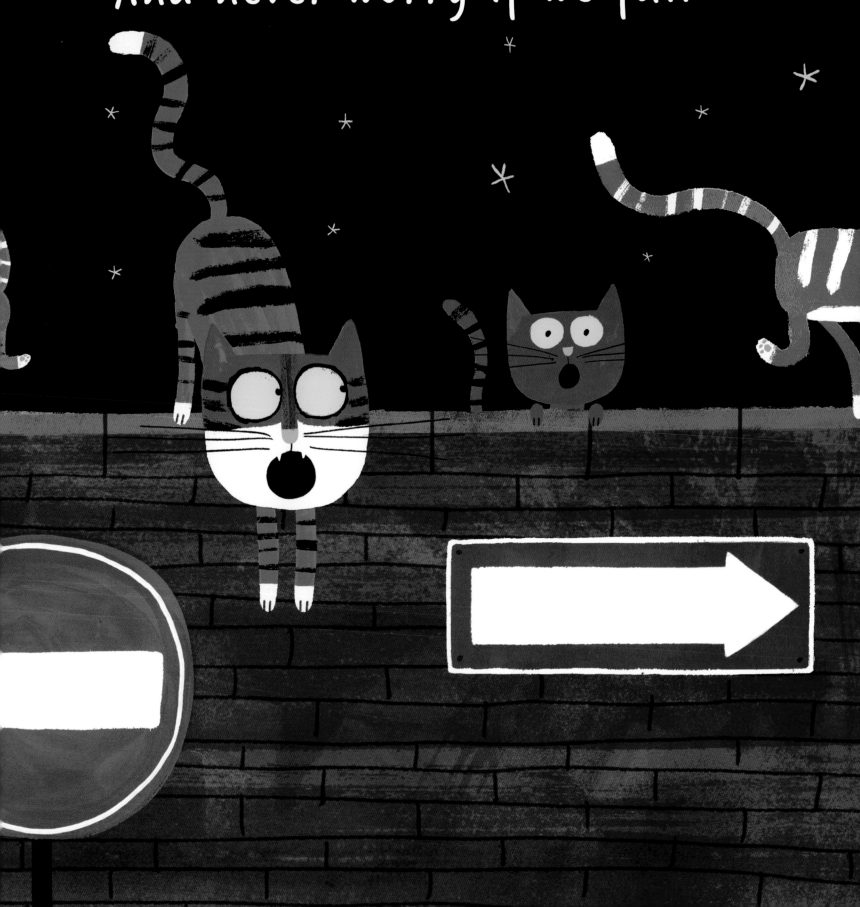

We'll **scare** the birds that roost about.

And see them put
the garbage out.

We'll hear the babies
cry and shout
And then we'll see
the sun come out.

And all too soon
there is no moon . . .

For when
it's morning
in the city . . .